UPDOG

WORLD'S GROSSEST

WORLD'S GROSSEST HISTORY FACTS

Scott Nickel

Lerner Publications ◆ Minneapolis

Lerner Publications Company
An imprint of Lerner Publishing Group, Inc.
241 First Avenue North
Minneapolis, MN 55401 USA

For reading levels and more information, look up this title at www.lernerbooks.com.

Main body text set in ITC Franklin Gothic Std.
Typeface provided by Adobe Systems.

Designer: Mary Ross

Library of Congress Cataloging-in-Publication Data

Names: Nickel, Scott, author.
Title: World's grossest history facts / Scott Nickel.
Description: Minneapolis: Lerner Publications, 2022. | Series: World's grossest (Updog books) | Includes bibliographical references and index. | Audience: Ages 8–11 | Audience: Grades K–1 | Summary: "Travel back in time to the gross old days. Readers will uncover the Great Stink of 1858, how doctors diagnosed patients by drinking their urine, and more!"—Provided by publisher.
Identifiers: LCCN 2020009439 (print) | LCCN 2020009440 (ebook) | ISBN 9781728403991 (library binding) | ISBN 9781728418957 (ebook)
Subjects: LCSH: Curiosities and wonders—Juvenile literature. | Science—Miscellanea—Juvenile literature. | History—Miscellanea—Juvenile literature.
Classification: LCC AG243 .N525 2021 (print) | LCC AG243 (ebook) | DDC 032.02—dc23

LC record available at https://lccn.loc.gov/2020009439
LC ebook record available at https://lccn.loc.gov/2020009440

Manufactured in the United States of America
1-48457-48971-6/8/2021

TABLE OF CONTENTS

THE GROSS OLD DAYS

The past was disgusting. People smeared poop on cuts and soaked clothes in pee.

In ancient Roman public toilets, everyone used the same sponge to wipe.

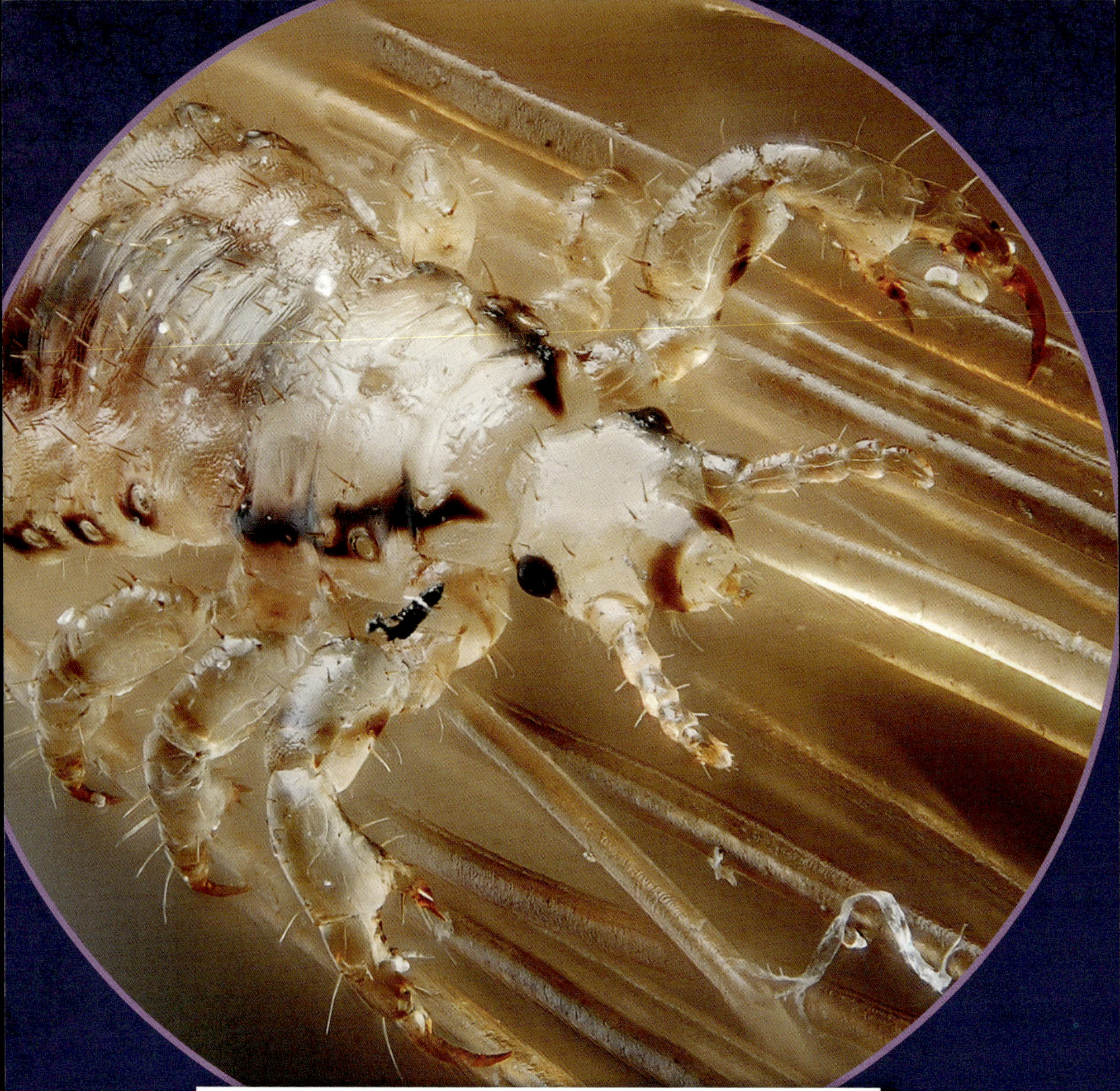

Lice were everywhere. To avoid them, people shaved their heads and wore wigs.

Plague-carrying fleas feasted on rats. Then the rats spread disease.

PLAGUE:
a disease that can cause death

UP NEXT!

STRANGE CURES.

BAD MEDICINE

For thousands of years, doctors thought bloodletting cured the sick.

BLOODLETTING: draining blood from a person

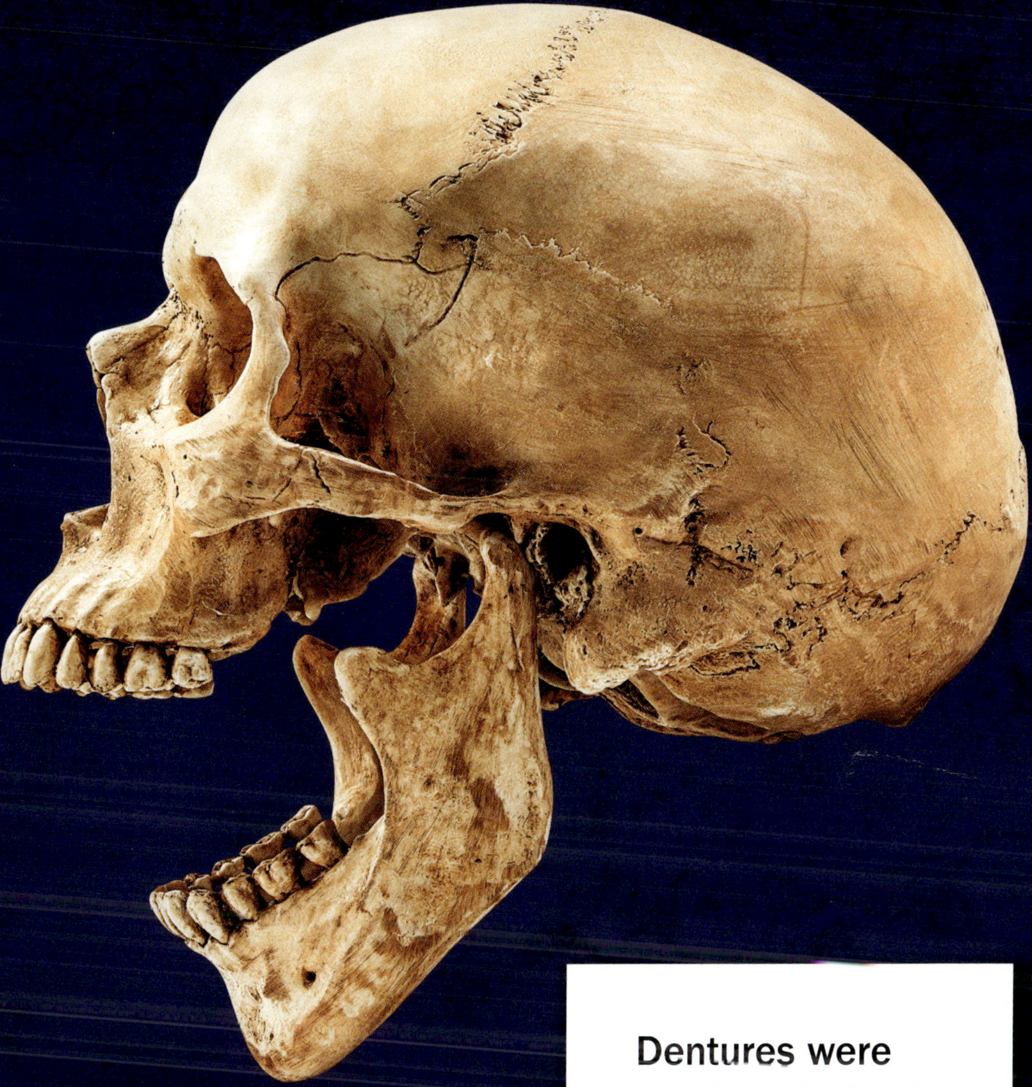

Dentures were made with dead people's teeth.

DENTURES: replacement teeth

WHICH IS GROSSER?

Animal Dung Ointments vs. Gladiator Blood

Ancient Egyptians used animal dung as medicine.

Drinking gladiator blood was believed to restore health.

GLADIATOR:
a fighter in ancient Rome

Medieval doctors drank their patients' urine to diagnose them.

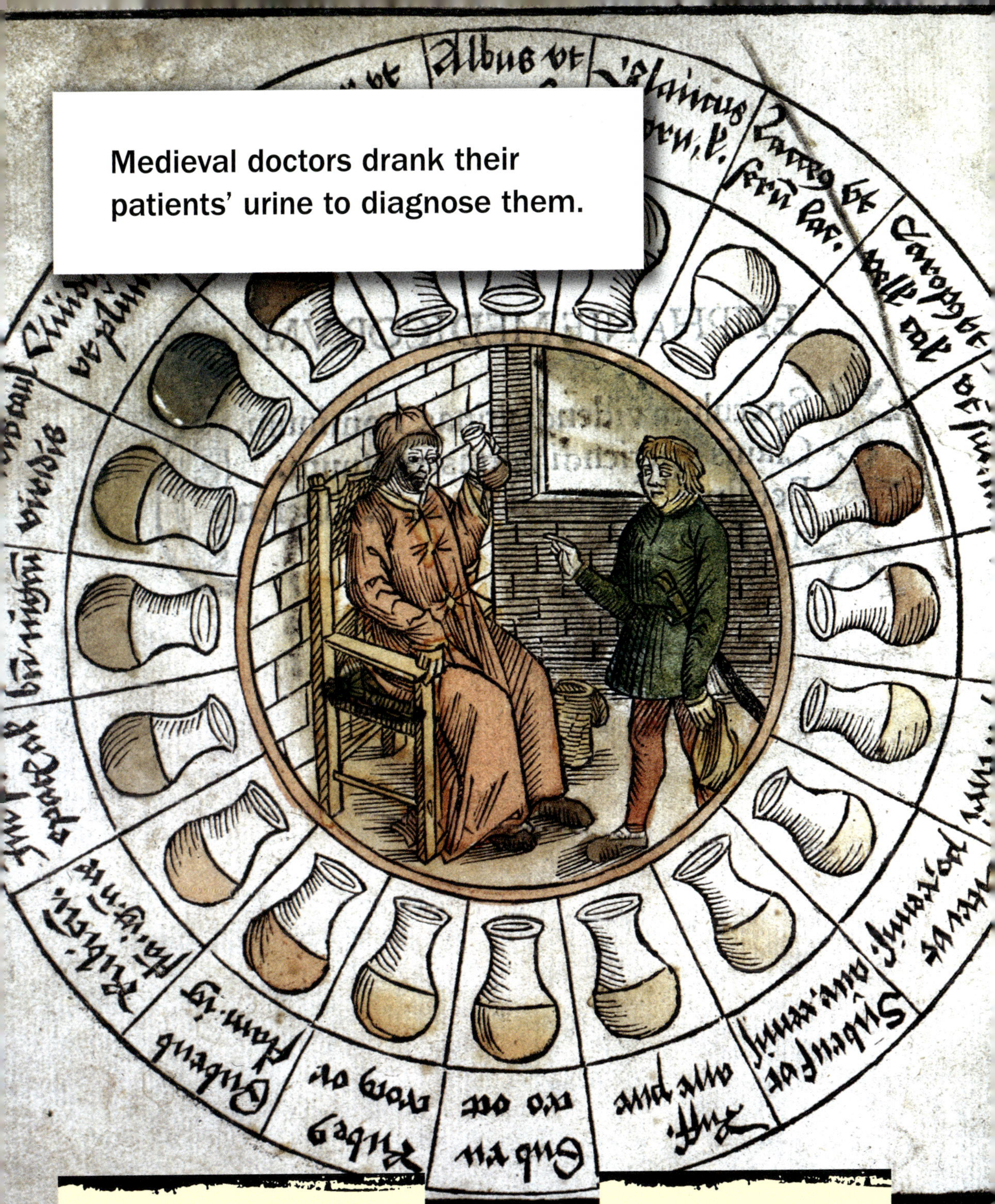

MEDIEVAL:
a historical period from about 500 to 1500

DIAGNOSE:
to recognize a disease or illness

DISGUSTING DIAGRAM!

Leeches suck blood. Doctors stuck them on patients to remove "bad" blood.

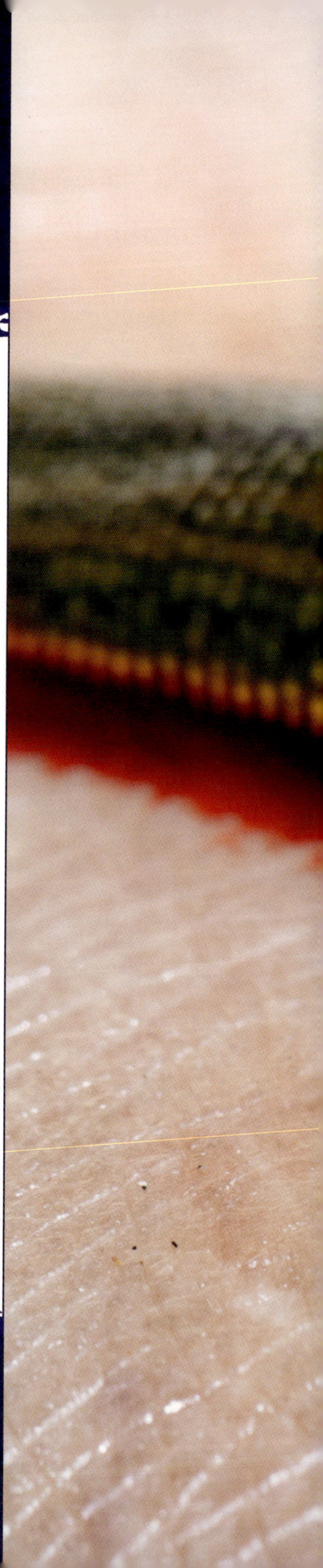

body
head
blood
sucker

Some ancient Greeks feasted on dirt and clay.

In London, sewage poured into a river. A hot summer heated up the sewage to create the Great Stink of 1858.

UP NEXT!

HORRIBLE HOUSEWORK.

UNCLEAN CLEANING

People often bathed in the Nile River. But they had to watch out for crocodiles and human waste.

Urine was used to clean clothes.

Few Roman homes had toilets. People emptied chamber pots out their windows.

CHAMBER POT: a bowl kept in the home for poop and pee

Smelly animal blood and guts littered the streets.

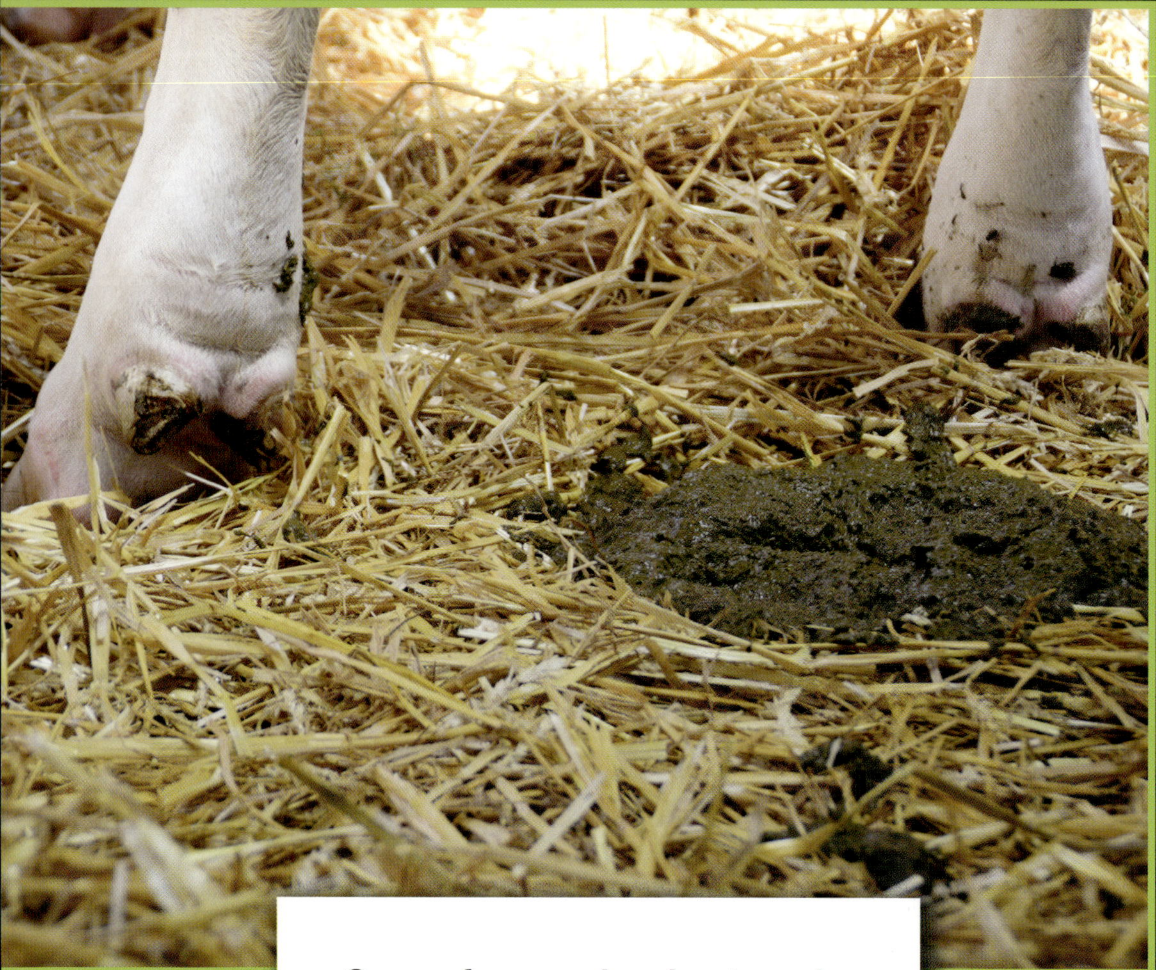

Some farm animals stayed indoors with families. They used straw floors as a toilet.

Those living in castles dumped their waste in the moat. History was never dull, but it was pretty gross.

Glossary

bloodletting: draining blood from a person

chamber pot: a bowl kept in the home for poop and pee

dentures: replacement teeth

diagnose: to recognize a disease or illness

gladiator: a fighter in ancient Rome

medieval: a historical period from about 500 to 1500

plague: a disease that can cause death

Check It Out!

History for Kids
https://www.historyforkids.net

Kiddle: Great Stink Facts
https://kids.kiddle.co/Great_Stink

National Geographic Kids: Gross Facts
https://kids.nationalgeographic.com/explore/13-facts-to-gross-out-your-parents

Nickel, Scott. *World's Grossest Human Body Facts.* Minneapolis: Lerner Publications, 2022.

Olexa, Keith. *The Gross Science of Lice and Other Parasites.* New York: Rosen, 2019.

Parvis, Sarah. *This Book Will Gross You Out.* New York: Downtown Bookworks, 2022.

Index

Photo Acknowledgments

Image credits: The J. Paul Getty Museum, Los Angeles, pp. 4, 17; shankar s./flickr (CC BY 2.0), p. 5; Gilles San Martin/Wikimedia Commons (CC BY-SA 2.0), p. 6; Carlos Aranguiz/Shutterstock.com, p. 7; Wellcome Library/Wikimedia Commons (CC BY 4.0), pp. 8, 11; fotoslaz/Shutterstock.com, p. 9; Metropolitan Museum of Art (public domain), p. 10 (left); MR. PRAWET THADTHIAM/Shutterstock.com, p. 10 (right); frank60/Shutterstock.com, p. 13; withGod/Shutterstock.com, p. 14; leo_photo/Shutterstock.com, p. 15; Stefan Scherer-Emunds/Shutterstock.com, p. 16; Chris Fithall/flickr (CC BY 2.0), p. 18; Rijksmuseum, Amsterdam, p. 19; NivCube/Shutterstock.com, p. 20; Jim Linwood/flickr (CC BY 2.0), p. 21. Design elements: Saravudh Sudkhaw/Shutterstock.com; Green angel/Shutterstock.com.

Cover: Wellcome Collection/Wikimedia Commons (CC BY 4.0).